Rachel's Changes

Angela Anwyl

authorHOUSE

AuthorHouse™ UK
1663 Liberty Drive
Bloomington, IN 47403 USA
www.authorhouse.co.uk
Phone: 0800.197.4150

© 2019 Angela Anwyl. All rights reserved.

No part of this book may be reproduced, stored in a retrieval system, or transmitted by any means without the written permission of the author.

Published by AuthorHouse   03/27/2019

ISBN: 978-1-7283-8667-6 (sc)
ISBN: 978-1-7283-8668-3 (e)

Print information available on the last page.

Any people depicted in stock imagery provided by Getty Images are models, and such images are being used for illustrative purposes only.
Certain stock imagery © Getty Images.

This book is printed on acid-free paper.

Because of the dynamic nature of the Internet, any web addresses or links contained in this book may have changed since publication and may no longer be valid. The views expressed in this work are solely those of the author and do not necessarily reflect the views of the publisher, and the publisher hereby disclaims any responsibility for them.

Review of Rachel Barrowovski

It is highly imaginative, with unexpected turns. I love the author's writing style, very kid oriented but with challenging vocabulary and subtle humour. I particularly enjoyed the descriptions of the teachers and just generally how the author sees things through a kid's eyes. There is a heartwarming underlying message of friendship and acceptance.

-Carol Bratina, Canadian Reader

Contents

Chapter 1	Rachel's secret	1
Chapter 2	Ivan Barrowovski	4
Chapter 3	Rachel's New Life	9
Chapter 4	Ivan's search	14
Chapter 5	A fun day out	17
Chapter 6	Wanda the Wonder Girl	21
Chapter 7	All the fun of the Fair	26
Chapter 8	Mulberry Cottage	31
Chapter 9	The Fair in Springtime	36
Chapter 10	The end of Wanda	39
Chapter 11	Together at last	42

Chapter 1

Rachel's secret

Rachel Smith-Hyde was 10 years old. She did all the usual things that 10 year old girls love to do. She and her 11 year old step-sister, Astrid, would search *U Tube* for *Try Not to Laugh* clips which always ended with them rolling on the floor in fits of the giggles. Astrid found the ones where people fell or tripped the funniest, whereas Rachel preferred the funny animal clips. They both learned all the latest dances and knew every word of every pop song. They loved to shop and whereas Astrid favoured frilly pink skirts and dresses, Rachel always chose leisure clothes, with Jack Wills being her absolute favourite.

But Rachel was not like other 10 year old girls – oh no! OK, so she worked hard at school and was always top in every test they took. She was brilliant at hockey and the only reason that she wasn't Captain of Hockey was because that honour always went to a Year 8 student and Rachel was only in Year 6. She looked forward to athletics in the summer term, knowing that she would outrun, out jump and out throw everyone.

Rachel was different because she had a secret – a BIG secret.

Rachel Smith-Hyde had been called Rachel Barrowovski until she was 'adopted' by Pops and Mims Smith-Hyde and their daughter, Astrid. When we say 'adopted', it hadn't been done officially, because officially, Rachel did not exist. All this is part of Rachel's secret. Of course the Smith-Hydes shared the secret.

Astrid had been in the same class as Rachel in a school in the hills of Cumbria. They had not been friends at first. In fact, Rachel didn't have any friends until, well, until her classmates discovered part of Rachel's secret. It had all come to light during a cross country race when there was a sudden downpour. All the children were soaked in seconds but something much worse happened to Rachel. As the rain seeped into her, Rachel began to jerk, smoke plumed from her t-shirt and she collapsed. The classmates had watched in amazement as it dawned on them why Rachel had appeared to be so much quicker and cleverer than they were – she was a robot and the rain had caused her mechanics to short-circuit. The children kept Rachel's secret to themselves because she won many prizes for the class.

Over time, Rachel became much loved by her classmates. By then she had many friends and invited them over to her house for a party As they had arrived,

Rachel's father along with a very unpleasant teacher, who had been their class 3 form teacher and was known as Sharp the Shark because of the way she snapped at the children, was shouting at her mother as they left in a hurry. Unbeknownst to the other children both Rachel and her 'mum' were quickly wearing out and the angry man was leaving them to rust and rot away.

Luckily for Rachel she was discovered and rescued by Astrid and her parents. Astrid's dad was a Professor in Robotics at Lancaster University and so was able to restore Rachel. Unfortunately he couldn't mend Rachel's mum and so they took Rachel to live with them. Shortly afterwards both Mr and Mrs Smith-Hyde got new jobs near London so the whole family moved.

Chapter 2

Ivan Barrowovski

Going back several years, a man called Ivan Barrowovski had come to England to make his fortune. All his life he had been building robots and hoped to become very rich by doing this. But some big companies in Russia had double crossed him and stolen his ideas.

So Ivan had gone to England with a plan to make lots of money and then to get revenge on the double crossing companies. His plan had been to take over several independent schools in England and to steal all their money. He had built Rachel and enrolled her in Hilltop School in the north of England. At first it had started well. He became Chair of Governors and so had the opportunities to gradually steal the money. But then it all went wrong. Rachel became popular – Ivan didn't know how that happened. She also became kind – that shouldn't have happened either. The Headteacher had

Rachel's Changes

started to suspect something and so Ivan and his side kick Hilda Sharp decided that it was time to move on.

As time passed, Ivan tried to build more robots but they were never as good as Rachel had been. He also found that he actually missed having Rachel around. Hilda Sharp was a miserable woman who constantly moaned about something or other. So Ivan took it into his head that he needed to get Rachel back.

"Pack zee cases, woman," he growled at Hilda, in his heavily accented English, one gloomy Monday morning, "We are going on zee trip."

Ivan had parked his limousine up for the time being – it was much too recognisable. He packed the cases into his new Volkswagen Golf – much more anonymous and they set off on the journey back up north to Cumbria.

Parking his car, outside the beloved little house, 'The Dacha' that Ivan and robot builders had constructed just a few years previously, Ivan and Hilda walked up the steps to the door, confident that although Rachel would surely be at school, her 'mother' would be at home.

Ivan did not knock on the door. It was his house after all. "'Ello," he boomed into the emptiness – nothing.

"'Ello," he called again as he made his way through the kitchen into the room behind.

"Vere are you?" he called out as room by room he hurried through the house – no one, nothing. Ivan didn't even notice the dust that had gathered on his computers and robot parts. He did not even see the models that

Rachel and her friends had built at her party. All he noticed was that Rachel and her mum were not there.

Gloomily he returned to the kitchen where finally he did notice something different - a note that Professor Smith-Hyde had left for him when he had rescued Rachel:

March 8th

Dear Mr Barrowovski

I am leaving you this note to let you know that I found both your robots in a dreadful condition.

I am therefore removing them and will do my best to restore them.

Sincerely,
Prof. Smith-Hyde

Ivan read the note again and again. It was now October – 7 months since he left the Dacha and Rachel and her mum.

"Never mind," he thought, "I should soon be able to track down this Professor Smith-Hyde and get Rachel back where she belongs."

He soon discovered that the Professor lectured in Robotics at Lancaster University.

"So he theenk he can steal my robots anda make hees fortune."

Not wanting to be seen by anyone from Hilltop School from where he had stolen lots of money, Ivan and Hilda Sharp stayed put in the Dacha, finding some fish fingers and chips in the freezer for their dinner. It never crossed either of their minds to clean or tidy the house, nor even to change bed sheets that had been gathering dust for so long.

Early the next morning they headed the few miles south to Lancaster.

Parking his car he growled to Hilda, "You stay here."

Putting on his pleasant face he entered the main building and approached the Receptionist.

"Good morning Madam," he smiled, "I have an appointment with Professor Smith-Hyde."

"I don't think you have," came the sharp reply.

Ivan saw red. "Do you call me a liar?" he spluttered

"I most certainly do," replied the Receptionist, "Professor Smith-Hyde left this University in June, so there is no way you have an appointment," she finished with a smug smile.

Ivan Barrowovski was not often lost for words but he was then. He stormed out, slamming the door so hard that the glass rattled and almost fell out.

"Shut up!" he screamed at Hilda Sharp before she had a chance to open her mouth.

The little car screeched out of the car park, through the town and onto the motorway in no time.

Gradually, Ivan calmed down and began to think. He must find out where this Professor had gone to. Had he taken his beloved Rachel with him? (Ivan had forgotten that Rachel meant nothing more to him than to help him make money). He pulled in to the next Motorway Services and Googled 'Professor Smith-Hyde'. Several headings came up, the most recent one telling him that.

> *Professor Smith-Hyde has just taken up the Chair of Robotics at Kings College University in London.*
>
> *For the past ten years he has worked as part of a team developing the subject at the University of Lancaster.*
>
> *He has a wife and two daughters, Astrid and Rachel..................*

"Rachel, Rachel," yelled Barrowovski. "He has a daughter called Rachel!"

Hilda had rushed into the café and returned with a carton of coffee. "Here you are, my love," she smiled at him, "Drink this and calm down. We will find her." Ivan growled in reply but drank his coffee as he thought out his next move.

Chapter 3

Rachel's New Life

In August, Rachel and her new family, Pops, Mims and Astrid had moved into their lovely new home, Mulberry Cottage, just a short walk away from the girls' new school, Southfields. The family had moved to a little village in Kent so that Pops could travel daily by train to his work in London and Mims could easily drive to her new job at the University of Kent in Canterbury.

In September both girls joined Year 6. What a great school Southfields was! The girls' favourite activity was the Wednesday afternoon 'Choices Time'. Both Astrid and Rachel chose to try horse riding from the amazing stables that they had noticed on their visit to the school. They happily spent an hour cleaning out the stables so as to have half an hour riding the gentle horses. Although neither of them had ridden before they soon found it a most relaxing way to see the countryside around the school.

They often bumped into Mr Warm, the jolly, smiling

headteacher, who obviously enjoyed his work with all the children. He knew the names of all the students in the school and would chat to them about how their lessons were going.

The pupils welcomed both girls even though Rachel seemed to be so much cleverer than they were. They figured that if her older sister didn't mind, why should they. They liked the fact that the new girls were cheerful and friendly and happy to join in class activities. Every break time, Rachel would join a group of children, mainly boys, for a game of football, whilst Astrid would seek out the girls huddled in a corner looking at the latest Pop magazines. Both girls really enjoyed their lessons. Rachel was on top form again and Astrid was proud of her 'sister'. No one had the slightest suspicion that the new family hid a massive secret.

Rachel's brilliance at all sports had soon been recognised by her new teachers and within the first month she had become the leading scorer of the hockey team.

The Smith-Hyde family enjoyed living in a new part of the country. Whilst the weather was still good they explored the countryside of Kent and the little seaside towns of Sussex. Wherever they drove, orchards of fruit were being picked. They often stopped to buy lovely fresh apples, pears and cherries to finish off their picnics. Astrid's favourite outing was to Conquest Bay where she would enjoy paddling in the chilly autumn waters. Rachel never joined her in these dips. Do you remember that Rachel could not get wet? Instead Rachel preferred pottering

Rachel's Changes

around the nearby town of Battle and visiting the site of the Battle of Hastings. She was especially thrilled when Pops took them there on October 14th – the very day of the Battle, all those hundreds of years ago.

Rachel and Astrid had kept in touch by *Facebook* with some of their friends from Hilltop School and they had been surprised to hear that amongst other good gossip, that the old Chair of Governors had disappeared some time ago, at the same time as that dragon of a teacher, Sharp the Shark. Wasn't the Chair of Governors Rachel's father? The family agreed that it was best not to respond to these questions. They didn't really want people to know that Rachel was not officially a Smith-Hyde, nor that she was living with them.

Even knowing that Ivan Barrowovski had moved away from Cumbria, the family were not prepared for what happened one gloomy Saturday in November.

Once the weather had turned cooler, Pops declared that on the next free Saturday, they would all take the train 'up to town' (meaning into London). And so it was that they set off good and early for a day in the city. The girls were most excited and talked about all the sights they wanted to see, "Madame Tussaud's", called Astrid. "The Tower of London" chose Rachel. "Oh, and Harrods of course" added Mims.

Pops laughed, "Fortunately, Harrods and Madame Tussaud's are close together so we can do those first, then we'll take the Tube to the Tower and have lunch in Covent Garden before we go to the theatre this afternoon.

Astrid just loved mingling with all the famous people in Madame Tussaud's Wax Museum. The girls took 'selfies' of themselves with the Royal Family, with the Beckhams, Usain Bolt, Jess Ennis-Hill and many more. Despite the fun they had there – remembering Rachel's famous party when all their class from Hilltop had made models – Rachel's favourite part of the museum was the *Stardome*, where you could explore the planets.

Next stop, Harrods, the world famous department store. Unfortunately for the family, most of the products on sale were rather too expensive for them but Mims bought a jar of marmalade in the Food Hall, the girls bought a tube of lip salve each and Pops splashed out on a can of shaving foam. Of course, they had all wanted to buy *something*, just so that they got one of the famous dark green bags in which to carry their purchase.

Armed with these precious bags, Pops guided his family to nearby Sloane Square, where they were to take the Central Line of the Tube to Tower Hill. The girls were amazed by how deep the Underground trains ran. On the platform they looked around in wonder, imagining what it must have been like in World War 2 when hundreds of people slept on these platforms night after night to avoid the German bombs that rained down on their city. Rachel nudged Astrid and pointed to a little mouse, calmly nibbling on a titbit beside the train tracks. Mims followed their gaze and boomed to all the waiting passengers that about half a million mice lived in the Underground System; there were murmurs of surprise from the passengers as a train whooshed into the station.

"We'll have a quick look at the outside of the Tower today," explained Pops, "But we haven't got time for a proper visit today. I'm sorry Rachel," he apologised, noticing her disappointment. "We will come again soon, I promise." Little did he know that he would not be able to keep this promise for a long time.

After a quick look at the imposing Tower of London, admiring the Beefeaters in their bright red uniforms and hearing the story of how if the ravens ever left the Tower, then England would be defeated, they zoomed off to grab a quick lunch before heading for a matinee show at the London Palladium.

Three hours later and still smiling from the amazing show in the stunningly beautiful theatre, the happy family emerged from the warmth of the theatre into a gloomy early evening. As they walked down the front steps, Rachel suddenly stopped in fear. There, in front of her stood a huge man with dark, dark hair………..

"Pops!" she shouted, recognising Ivan Barrowovski at once. Pops saw her fright, grabbed her and bundled his family into a waiting taxi. "Charing Cross Station, FAST" he yelled at the driver.

Chapter 4

Ivan's search

Back in October, having stormed away from the University in Lancaster, Ivan had sat in his Golf in the car park of the Service Station on the M6 and thought;

"So Smith-Hyde has taken my girl to London. Then that ees where I must go to find her."

Ivan Barrowovski had never been to London and didn't realise just what an impossible task that would be. He thought that London would be just a little bit bigger than Lancaster. How wrong he was.

He did realise that he would be able to search easier on his own so he shooed Hilda Sharp back to the Dacha. "Anda mek sure you cleen eet," he insisted.

Hilda Sharp was not happy with this decision, "But at least I'll have somewhere to live," she reasoned.

Having made his decision Ivan set off happily, to drop Hilda at the nearest train station, before he continued southwards towards London.

Rachel's Changes

Two days later, Ivan was exhausted. He had walked for miles looking for Rachel. He had slept under a bridge and people were starting to look at him strangely because he was dirty and scruffy and rather smelly. Ivan could now see that his search wasn't going to be as easy as he had first thought. And so he set about finding a flat to rent. Although he had plenty of fake money, he didn't know how long he would have to make it last so he looked for a cheap flat in a central area. He took the Tube to Covent Garden. He liked this station because it had lifts instead of escalators so he thought he'd look around that area for somewhere to sleep. It took all day but eventually he found a tiny bedsit that cost a fortune but at least he could sleep in a bed and wash and clean up there.

Ivan's life took on a new pattern. Every morning he would get up, wash, shave and head out for breakfast at a coffee shop. Then he would wander the streets of London, looking, always looking. By late evening he would return to his tiny bedsit just waiting to start his search the next day.

He lost track of the days and the weeks but the weather was beginning to turn cooler. One day he had wandered as far as the Tower of London and decided to treat himself to a visit. As he was passing the Beefeaters on his way in he caught a glimpse of a young girl. For one minute he held his breath but then he saw the girl join her family of two brothers so knew he was mistaken. He found the visit to the Tower really interesting. He had never visited anywhere so old before. He decided to have an early night for a change, but as he headed home, passing the Palladium, crowds of laughing people were just leaving the matinee performance, suddenly, right in front of him stood.................. Rachel!

"Pops!" she had cried.

Ivan was just about to reach out for her when all four leapt into a waiting taxi. The last thing Ivan heard was the man shouting, "Charing Cross Station. Fast."

Knowing he couldn't catch up with them for now, Ivan hurried back to the warmth of his flat to re-think his plan.

By morning, he had worked out that obviously the family did not live in London but took the train in. He checked on his computer to find where trains went to from Charing Cross Station. That wasn't a great help because he could see that the station served a big area of Kent. He thought and thought and then thought a bit more.

"If the family don't live in London, the maybe they come in to the city to see the sights at the weekends." With an evil grin, he knew what he had to do – spend Saturdays and Sundays at Charing Cross Station. This was going to be a whole lot easier than tramping the streets.

Chapter 5

A fun day out

Several weeks passed after the scare that the Smith-Hyde family had outside the Palladium. Life was busy for Pops at the University in London and Mims at her University of Kent. The girls worked hard at school and Rachel was also busy playing hockey whenever she could. From time to time, Pops would adjust Rachel's computers. He wanted to keep her in tip-top condition.

The girls heard on *Facebook* that Sharp the Shark had returned to teach at Hilltop School and was as horrid as ever.

This news came as a pleasant surprise to Rachel, "If she's back there, then she and Ivan must have gone back to the Dacha." With that relief in her mind she hurried off to ask Pops and Mims if they could have another trip to London, now that they knew it was safe.

And so it was, that on a cold December Sunday, the family once again headed off to London. As they arrived in Charing Cross station the girls were so excitedly talking about where they were going to visit that no one noticed the large, dark haired man, watching them from behind his newspaper.

And what a busy day they had. They decided to take an open topped, hop on/hop off double decker bus. First stop had been the Natural History Museum where they all gasped in amazement at the skeleton of a huge blue whale suspended above them. When they had had their fill of animated dinosaurs and visited an earthquake simulator they all decided that the next stop should be the Tate Modern Art Gallery. Whilst Mims drooled over Picasso's, Dali's and Andy Warhol's, the girls giggled at some of the weird and wonderful works of modern art.

They all agreed that the next stop must be the Science Museum. They knew there were loads of hands-on activities. They were amazed by one of the earliest mobile phones – it was huge and by a 500 year old artificial arm. Rachel was particularly interested in that, knowing that both of hers were actually artificial. Pops was surprised to discover that the Queen had sent her first tweet on Twitter from this Museum.

As they left the Science Museum it was getting dark and by now they had red noses and blue fingers from the cold on top of the buses so Pops suggested a taxi ride to see the Christmas Decorations before they headed back home.

They sat back in the taxi and enjoyed the magnificent

Rachel's Changes

lights on Oxford Street, down Regent Street and into Covent Garden.

Four sleepy Smith-Hydes sank back in the taxi as it headed back to Charing Cross Station.

Ivan had not followed the family around London that day. Oh no! He knew that they would return to the station at the end of the day and so he stayed put and plotted.

He had stolen a uniform from the railway workers staffroom and when dressed in it looked oh so different with his dark hair hidden beneath the cap. He had hired a taxi and had it waiting, engine running, at the side entrance to the station. Now all he had to do was patiently wait.

The day passed slowly. The light began to fade and darkness fell. Ivan was beginning to worry that he had missed them when suddenly, there they were.

As they approached the barrier, he called, "Hurry, the train is about to leave."

As they all started to run he grabbed Rachel, putting his enormous hand over her mouth so that she couldn't make a sound and carrying her, ran in the opposite direction towards the waiting taxi. "Go!" he wheezed to the taxi driver.

Meanwhile, what of Rachel's family? They had leapt onto the train puffing and laughing after their dash to catch the train. It would have been an hour's wait until the next one.

"Rachel," boomed Mims, "where is Rachel?" As the train gathered speed they looked at one another in horror. What had happened to Rachel?

Astrid suddenly went pale, "That guard who told us to hurry looked awfully familiar. I think it might have been Rachel's father."

It all began to make sense – seeing Ivan Barrowovski outside the Palladium, Pops shouting 'Charing Cross Station' to the taxi driver. Ivan Barrowovski had known which station they used.

He had snatched Rachel back.

"We must call the police, immediately," bellowed Mims.

"How can we," replied Pops sadly, "she doesn't exist."

"She will get back to us," confidently thought Astrid, "After all, she is my sister."

Chapter 6

Wanda the Wonder Girl

In the taxi on their way to Covent Garden, Ivan was so happy to have his Rachel back with him. He kept telling her how much he loved her and had missed her. A sullen Rachel was not taken in by this change to the man who had only been unkind to her, "You never loved me, you only used me. You only built me to do your dirty tricks."

By the end of the journey, Ivan had realised that she was right. She could be of use to him again.

He was impressed by the work that Smith-Hyde had done on Rachel. She was in very good shape and as she answered every one of his questions, a plan began to form.

Pretending to care about her and that he wanted them to be together and not have to go back to Hilda Sharp who was staying at the Dacha, Ivan shared his cunning plan with Rachel:

"We weel join a travelling Fair," he told her. "That way we weel have somewhere to live and we weel get to see the country. It'll be good fun."

"What will we do?" asked Rachel. "Why would a fair want us?"

"Because we have something that no other fair has. We have Wanda ze Wonder Girl."

"We do? Who is she?"

"It ees you my clever girl," replied Ivan. "You can answer anyone's questions about anything."

Day after day, Ivan would disappear, leaving Rachel on her own in the tiny bedsit. Rachel would sit at the window, looking out onto the square, watching Christmas shoppers scurrying to and fro and hoping to see Pops who must be searching for her. There was no phone in the flat so she could not ring them to tell them she was safe and Ivan always locked her in when he went out. She was his prisoner.

Finally, Ivan came back in a very good mood. "I have joined us up with a travelling fair," he told Rachel. "We leave tomorrow. Here, make yourself look exotic," as he threw a bag at her. Rachel looked in the bag and found bright red hair dye and brilliantly colourful clothes decorated with bells and mirrors.

The next day, Ivan and the unusual looking girl, left the Covent Garden flat and took a train journey of about an hour, followed by another hour's walk until they reached

Rachel's Changes

some waste land. In the centre was a large tent, surrounded by caravans, some very modern, some incredibly old and some beautifully decorated with bright flowers. Ivan led Rachel to a small, dirty looking caravan and handed her a key, "Our new home," he proudly pronounced. Rachel shuddered when she thought of the lovely houses she had lived in with the Smith-Hydes. She must find a way to escape.

Ivan took Rachel to explore the Fairground. He explained that instead of the fairground being in the open air, in winter time, they use the big old circus tent. Entering through the large flap, Rachel gasped at the flurry of activity inside. Wherever she looked people were putting up rides in the centre of the tent. Round the edges were smaller stalls. Ivan proudly pointed out what was going on:

"Over there, ees ze Bumping Cars, there ze 'Elter Skelter, 'ere weel be ze Fun Slide but ze very best is over 'ere." He lead Rachel round the Bumping Cars to where a group of men were busily putting together the most beautiful Carousel she had ever seen. The horses were different colours, cream, grey, brown, black with white patches, pure white, all with gleaming leather saddles and harnesses and decorated with real gold paint. Rachel loving stroked a black and white horse, "Hello Dobbin," she whispered, "Will you be my friend?"

"Eh up luv!" called one of the workers, "We're not open yet and how did you know he was called Dobbin?"

"Oh" laughed Rachel, "I just knew and I'm going to be with the Fair too."

"Oh aye, I've heard that one before. Now be off with you."

"You sillee man," boomed Ivan Barrowovski. "Zees ees Wanda the Wonder Girl. Did she not know the name of your 'orse?"

The workman looked a bit confused but wasn't easily frightened by the big, dark man.

"Oh aye and what's my name if you know everything then?"

Rachel laughed and whispered to Ivan. She was beginning to enjoy this after all.

"Goodbye Peter," called Ivan as they left the open mouthed workman behind.

Just across from the Carousel, Ivan stopped again and pointed out a stall to Rachel. Behind a wooden counter was set up what looked a bit like a little living room – two comfortable chairs with a small coffee table between them. On the walls were photographs of famous people – actors, pop stars, even a member of the Royal Family. Rachel looked confused.

"Zees ees our stall," explained Ivan. "I sit 'ere," he pointed at a stool by the wooden counter. "I take ze money and watch ze people. You sit 'ere," he indicated one of the comfy chairs, "Ze people they come anda ask you ze question."

"Is that all?" replied Rachel. "But why are all those photos on the wall?"

Ivan laughed his horrid laugh, "Zey have all beena

your customers." Rachel knew that this obviously wasn't true. It was Ivan being false yet again.

He led her back to the front of the stall and proudly indicated a sign waiting to be put up.

> # WANDA THE
> # WONDER GIRL

Chapter 7

All the fun of the Fair

Rachel was impressed. Despite not wanting to be there, despite not wanting to be anywhere with Ivan, despite missing her family, she had to admit to herself that this could be fun, for a while anyway.

They continued their tour around the fairground stopping to look at the Coconut Shy, where Ivan explained that you had 3 wooden balls to try to knock a coconut off a stand. If you did, you got to keep the coconut. Ivan happily also explained that the coconuts were sitting in Blu Tack which made them harder to knock off.

The next stall was 'Splat the Rat', just a drainpipe, a fabric 'rat' and a bat. The stall holder would drop the rat down the drainpipe. The customer would try to time it to hit the rat with the bat. If they did they could choose a prize from the display at the back of the stall. "Ees really hard," laughed Ivan.

"He really is a very nasty man," thought Rachel to herself.

Rachel's Changes

Next they came to a Hoopla stall where you could buy large wooden rings which you attempted to throw over prizes. "Ha," Ivan laughed his nasty laugh, "Feel how light the rings are. So hard to throw."

The final stall looked a bit like Rachel's but instead of the living room, it had red velvet curtains. They took a peek behind the curtains and in the space behind stood a circular table, covered in a red cloth and standing in the middle was a crystal ball.

Pulling Rachel outside the stall Ivan explained that this stall belonged to Madame Zushi – a fortune teller.

"Anda now we get you ready" said Ivan. "Ze fair opens tonight."

Back in the scruffy caravan, Ivan set about checking Rachel out. Hair now red, yes. Fancy clothes, yes. "Just one more theeng," he mumbled as he held Rachel's head in a tight grip and swiftly changed her bright blue eyes for a pair of brilliant green ones. "Now no one will recognise you."

By 6 o'clock in the evening, Rachel was in her comfy chair in her stall, enjoying listening to the carousel as she watched her friend Dobbin glide up and down, round and round. She could have felt quite content if it hadn't been that Ivan was sitting on the stool in front of her. As she sat there Rachel thought of her family. Would they be sad that she was missing? Would they be looking for her? What would school think about her having disappeared? Suddenly, Rachel gave a little giggle to herself. Here she was – Wanda the Wonder Girl, able to answer any question. So she closed her brilliant green eyes and thought,

'Would her family be sad that she was missing?' Rachel immediately got a picture in her mind of Pops, Mims and Astrid, sitting in the cosy lounge of Mulberry Cottage. No one was speaking, no one was smiling. Mims was looking at a photograph of Rachel. Pops was engrossed in looking at a map. Astrid was reading a book of Rachel's and had tears running gently down her cheeks. The answer – yes – her family was sad

'Would they be looking for her?' Again, Rachel closed the green eyes and this time, heard the voices of her family

"We can't go to the police," Pops was saying, "She doesn't officially exist"

"We must find that brute, Barrowovski. Then we'll locate our darling Rachel," uttered Mims in a surprisingly quiet voice.

All she could hear from Astrid were muffled sobs."

Rachel immediately felt some comfort. She knew her family would never forget her. Somehow, they would be together again.

Rachel's dreaming was suddenly interrupted by Ivan talking to someone about her and before she knew it a woman of about 40 was sitting opposite her.

"Hello Luv," smiled the woman. "That man says you can answer any question. Well, here's the thing. I'm all on my own and I'm not happy. I work in an office in town

Rachel's Changes

and it's so boring. All I do all day long is answer the phone and file bits of paper away.

My question to you is……What job should I do?"

Rachel looked carefully at the woman and slowly closed the bright green eyes. In her mind she could see the woman wearing a nurse's uniform. Opening her eyes she explained this to the woman who beamed a huge smile at Rachel, "That's it!" she cried. "I've always wanted to be a nurse but I know it will take me a while to train. I will do it."

And off she went, commenting to anyone who would listen that the Wonder Girl was truly wonderful.

In no time at all a queue had formed in front of Ivan. He beamed with pleasure as kerching, kerching, more and more money was paid into his cash box.

"How many children will I have?"

"Why is the sky blue?"

"What are the numbers for next weekend's lottery draw?"

"How can I make my fortune?"

"Which horse will win the Grand National?"

"I'm not feeling well, should I see a doctor?"

And so the evening passed in a flurry of questions with carousel music playing in the background. By 10 o'clock, Rachel was exhausted. For every customer she had a picture in her mind and told them just what she saw.

As the Fairground closed for the night, Ivan led a weary Rachel back to the dirty little caravan. As she fell asleep, Rachel promised herself that first thing in the morning she would clean and clean until the caravan sparkled.

Soon a pattern of her new life was set. In the mornings Rachel would scrub and polish until the little caravan began to feel a bit more like a home. Rachel would make time every day to visit her friend Dobbin, the wooden carousel horse. She would put her arms around him and whisper her hopes and fears to him. He always seemed to give her comfort, although he said nothing at all. In the afternoons a few people would venture into the large tent but it was the evenings that were the busiest. Every night Rachel answered question after question. Every few days, the workmen would take down the stalls and the tent and they would all travel for a few hours to a new site where once again the Fair was set up and the same pattern of her life continued. Rachel knew that Christmas had come and gone because there were no longer Christmas lights as they travelled to a new site but she had no idea what time of year it was, nor where in the country they were. People's accents changed but the questions never did. Wherever they were people always wanted to know how they could make more money. "Why are people so greedy?" wondered Rachel. "Why can't they see that money does not always make you happy?"

But she had only to take a look at Ivan. The money she was making for him certainly seemed to make him happy.

Chapter 8

Mulberry Cottage

Meanwhile, what of the Smith-Hyde family?

Well, just as Rachel had 'seen', the family were all so sad that Rachel wasn't with them. They felt so helpless. Making up a story for school that Rachel was not well and had gone to stay with relatives, poor Astrid was left to try to answer curious classmates and team members who wanted to know just what was wrong with her, she hadn't seemed ill, when was she coming back, was she going to another school whilst she was away? Astrid did all she could not to lie to her friends but it became harder and harder until eventually she would take a book to school and at break times, she would hide away, reading. She became very quiet and was very lonely.

Pops and Mims worried about Astrid as much as they did about Rachel. There seemed to be nothing they could do. At weekends Pops would travel back into London and search and search everywhere they could think of.

Suddenly, Mims had an idea and boomed, "I know

where she'll be! He will have taken her back to his house in Cumbria." The whole family realised that this was the most likely place for Rachel to be. After all, Ivan Barrowovski had all his equipment in that house didn't he? They knew that Rachel had not returned to Hilltop because Astrid still had *Facetime* messages from old friends. They knew that horrid Sharp the Shark had returned. Of course none of the family knew that Ivan Barrowovski had stolen money from the school and so was unlikely to go near the school.

They held a family meeting, trying to decide how they could get Rachel back from Barrowovski. He had built her originally and they actually had no claim on her.

"Could we reason with him that Rachel is better off with us?" wondered Mims.

"There is no reasoning with that man," replied Pops. "He didn't take proper care of her before. Do you remember how broken she was when we took her from his house?"

Mims and Astrid remembered it well. There had been a party at the Dacha which is where Rachel had lived. After the party, Rachel had not returned to school so eventually Astrid had told her parents all about Rachel and together they went to the little house in the woods. There they had found lifeless Rachel and her robot mum. Pops being a robotics expert had managed to repair Rachel but could not save her mum. That was how Rachel had come to live with them. Soon after that they had moved south to new jobs for Pops and Mims and had felt safely away from Barrowovski.

"How about we go up for a weekend and see how the land lies," suggested Astrid. "We can call in on some old friends whilst we are there."

"Good thinking," replied her parents.

And so it was that on a lovely spring Saturday the Smith-Hyde family set off bright and early for a trip back to Cumbria. It took a long time for them to drive around London but finally they were on the motorway, heading north. After a short stop for breakfast they all felt excited at the prospect of being reunited with Rachel very soon. They took turns to choose songs to sing and the miles melted away. Soon they were turning off the motorway and heading up to the Fells.

"Should we go straight to the Dacha?" asked Astrid

"I think so," replied her father, "We don't know how long it will take to persuade Barrowovski that Rachel is better off with us."

As the car pulled into the clearing in front of the little house, they were relieved to see the limousine that Barrowovski travelled in, parked up. Surprisingly, it looked very dusty and Pops noticed a flat tyre.

The family climbed out of their car, stretching their stiff legs. That had been a long drive. Now they just wanted to rescue Rachel and get out of there.

They climbed the steps in front of the house and

Mims rapped on the door.........No answer. She rapped again....... Still no answer. The family looked at one another in fear, remembering that previous visit when they had discovered Rachel and her mum slumped on the floor.

"Stay there," instructed Pops as he turned the door knob and walked in. Fortunately there was no Rachel lying on the floor but instead, lying on a sofa, snoring loudly lay Hilda Sharp.

Laughing, he went to the door and called Mims and Astrid in, "Come and look at this sight."

With an extra loud snort, Miss Sharp woke up and leapt to her feet, "What are you doing in my house?" she demanded.

Ignoring the fact that it wasn't actually her house, Pops explained that Rachel had been living with them because Barrowovski had not looked after her properly. Now they had come to take Rachel back again because she was much better off with them.

At that Hilda Sharp, the Shark that Astrid remembered only too well from her days at Hilltop School laughed her cruel laugh. "Well, you've wasted your journey then haven't you? She's not here. He's not here and I don't know nor care where either of them are. Last I heard he was heading to London to look for her."

The Smith-Hyde family looked at one another in dismay. They had come all this way for nothing. They had been so sure that Rachel would have been here. They sadly looked at each other.

"Should we go home?" asked Pops

Mims and Astrid sadly nodded. That journey took forever. No jolly songs. No stops for meals. Just 3 people all wondering what on earth they could do next to find their beloved Rachel.

Chapter 9

The Fair in Springtime

As the evenings gradually became lighter and the weather warmer, Rachel realised that she had been with the Fair for six months. More often than not, the workmen did not put up the big tent now but set up the Fair in the open air. The people who came to the Fair were now dressed in brightly coloured summer clothes. They seemed to laugh more and certainly were happy to spend more money. Rachel made sure that her stall was always close to the carousel. Every day she would chat to her friend Dobbin the carousel horse, asking him the one question that she had no answer to, "When will I go home?" Dobbin never answered but Rachel knew that she had one friend with her.

But Rachel was tired, oh so tired. She worked on her busy stall every afternoon and evening answering question after question and cleaned the little caravan every morning. Ivan Barrowovski was never there – he spent every spare minute with Madame Zushi, the Fortune

Rachel's Changes

Teller. Rachel even saw him wave and wink at her across the Fairground whilst he was sitting at the entrance to her stall! Rachel did not mind that he left her alone but she hadn't realised that she was so tired because he never had any time to adjust her computers nor to replace worn out parts. Rachel was slowly wearing out again. Barrowovski did not concern himself with keeping her in good shape. To him she was just a money making machine and she was making him a fortune!

One day, after a particularly long journey, the Fair arrived in a large field, covered in daisies. Rachel climbed down from the van that towed the old caravan and sniffed the air. The scent was wonderful. It smelt like……….. home! Rachel wondered where in England they were and why it smelled so familiar.

The workmen were already busily putting together the old Carousel. Rachel wandered over, smiling at them as she put her arms around Dobbin. "Isn't this place wonderful Dobbin. I wonder where we are." Yet again, Rachel could not answer her own question. If she had she would have been able to see that not many miles away, a mother and father were comforting their sad eleven year old daughter. They promised her a trip to a visiting Fair to cheer her up.

As soon as the Fair was up and ready, the gates were open and happy visitors streamed in. The Carousel was immediately busy, with the beautiful horses prancing up and down to the loud music. As always Wanda the

Wonder Girl soon had a queue of people waiting to ask her a question. Ivan Barrowovski beamed as the pound coins poured into his greedy hands and his bulging pockets.

It was getting towards the time when the Fair closed for the dinner hour, when a young girl paid her money and sat opposite Rachel. Rachel's green eyes opened wide in amazement. It was Astrid! She was actually here. Her family had come to rescue her.

Rachel glanced across at Ivan. He was glaring at Rachel and drew a finger threateningly across his throat warning her to say nothing, He had recognised Astrid but Astrid recognised neither him nor Rachel who looked so different in her fancy clothes, with dyed red hair and bright green eyes.

"On Wanda" breathed Astrid, "Please tell me, will I ever find my lost sister?"

"She is very close," whispered Rachel. "You will soon be together again."

An overjoyed Astrid leapt out of the chair and rushed to find her parents to share the wonderful news that Wanda the Wonder Girl had told her.

She and Mims and Pops were so thrilled to hear that Rachel wasn't far away and that they would soon be together that they did not see nor hear the commotion that was going on in a stall close to the Carousel.

Chapter 10

The end of Wanda

As Astrid ran out of her stall, Rachel smiled a gentle smile. She knew that she had answered Astrid's question correctly and that whatever Ivan Barrowovski did he would not be able to stop her going back to her beloved family.

"I'll see you soon," she whispered as she quietly slid to the floor.

Ivan did not notice at first that Rachel had collapsed. He was too busy watching the joyous Smith-Hyde family and wondered what they were so happy about. He was also busily taking in the money and blowing kisses to Madame Zushi.

He was miles away, when suddenly a man's angry voice brought him down to earth, "Hey Mister! This Wanda's no Wonder Girl. She's asleep on the floor."

Ivan rushed round the counter, pushing the man away and putting up a closed sign.

"Go away," he shouted, "Just go away!" The angry

customers who had paid their money wandered off, looking for someone to complain to.

Ivan looked at Rachel in a panic. She was totally worn out. Her computers had broken. She was useless.

Ivan waited until the Fair had closed for the night before he gathered up all his belongings, the bags and bags of money he had saved up and piling them into the car, silently drove away from the little caravan. He parked as close as he could to Wanda's stall and leaving the boot opened crept into the silent Fairground. He gathered the lifeless Rachel into his arms and scurried back to the waiting Golf, relieved that no one had spotted him. In fact he had been seen but no one saw the tears running down Dobbin the Carousel horse's face.

From that day on, Dobbin was rarely ridden because he looked so sad. If you ever see a Carousel, look for a sad, black and white horse – it might be Dobbin.

Ivan Barrowovski knew that he had to disappear again but first he had to get rid of the useless robot. Driving into a quiet town, Ivan spotted a narrow lane, almost blocked by a large orange skip. He pulled in and opening the boot just a little so as not to be noticed, dragged the lifeless Rachel out and bundled her behind the skip before driving off laughing to himself, "Free at last! Free of the robot girl and free from horrid Hilda. I wonder eef Madame Zushi would like to run away with me?"

Rachel's Changes

The next morning the owner of a junk shop on the narrow lane was putting some rubbish into the skip when he tripped over Rachel. Thinking at first that it was a dead body he shouted for his neighbours, "Quick, quick! I need help!"

Several other shop keepers dashed out and stood looking down at Rachel. Suddenly one of the women started to laugh, "You old fool, Reg. That's not a dead body. It's a dummy – you know, like ventriloquists have."

"I knew that," said Reg, his face going very red, "I was just tricking you. It's a good one isn't it."

Thinking that the dummy might make him some money, Reg lifted Rachel and carried her into his gloomy little shop, where he placed her on a chair in the window.

Chapter 11

Together at last

"That Wanda said that we were near to Rachel and that we'd soon be together," moaned Astrid. She was bored and lonely. It was the start of the summer holidays and the family had made no plans because they were forever searching for Rachel.

"Let's go to the seaside," Mims suggested. "Brighton would be fun. We can have a paddle and a wander round the antique shops. I would love a new, old chair for the lounge."

The family reluctantly set off. Nothing was fun anymore. But once in Brighton, Astrid did enjoy a paddle in the cold waters of the sea and having a giant ice cream before they escaped the heat of the midday by wandering into the cool, shady lanes that housed many antique shops. After an hour's wandering and Mims not finding any chair to take her fancy, they were all in need of a cup of tea before they set off for home. Mims spotted a café at the far end of a little alleyway. They hadn't gone more

Rachel's Changes

than a few yards down the alleyway when Astrid stopped in front of a junk shop window, "Look," she called to her parents. "Isn't that Wanda the Wonder Girl?" Her parents thought it might be as they continued on to the café.

As they sipped their tea and nibbled on buttered scones Pops and Mims could see that something was troubling Astrid. "What is it love?" queried Mims

"It's Wanda," sighed Astrid. "There's something not right."

The family returned to the little junk shop in the alleyway and stood staring at the 'dummy' in the window. They were just about to move on when Pops gasped, "Look at her," he shouted. "Really look." Mims and Astrid stared at Wanda but shrugged their shoulders.

"Imagine her hair was dark brown and her eyes were blue. Who would she look like?"

Suddenly the penny dropped, "It's Rachel! It's Rachel" they shrieked.

"Leave this with me," said Pops as he wandered into the shop.

"How much do you want for that, er, that thing in the window," he asked, trying not to sound too interested.

"Oh you mean my ventriloquist's dummy?" replied Reg the shop keeper. "She's very special. I couldn't let her go for less than £10."

"£5" offered Pops

"£7.50 and she's yours."

Reg and Pops shook hands on the deal and Pops gently lifted Rachel out of her chair and outside to a beaming Mims and Astrid.

"Can you fix her, Pops?" asked Astrid

"I'm not sure. She's in really bad shape – again. But I'll do my best."

It was with mixed feelings that the Smith-Hyde family returned to Mulberry Cottage. They were so happy to have Rachel back with them, where she belonged but worried that Pops may not be able to fix her.

Back at the Cottage they gently carried Rachel into Pops' workshop." Can we get her hair colour changed quickly?" asked Astrid. "I want her to start looking like our Rachel."

Mims told her that it would wash out in time so every day Astrid gently shampooed Rachel's hair until finally it was its original rich, brown colour.

"What about her eyes?"

"Leave it with me," laughed Pops.

Day after day, week after week all through the summer holidays Pops worked on Rachel's computers until one day at the beginning of September – on Astrid's birthday in fact – Rachel's (now blue) eyes opened with a 'ping'. "Hi Pops," she smiled before closing them again.

From that day they all knew that Rachel was going to be alright. Pops lovingly rebuilt her, making her look a little older. After all the girls were due to be going to a Senior School shortly.

Every day, Rachel was 'awake' for a bit longer and as

the autumn mists began to gather in the mornings and evenings, Pops and Mims called a family meeting.

"It's time to move on, girls," they stated. "Ivan Barrowovski has got a rough idea of where we are. You never know if he might come looking again, even though he doesn't know that we have you back, Rachel. He believes that Rachel is broken. But we can't risk losing you again."

The girls nodded in agreement. Somehow Mulberry Cottage had lost some of its' charm when Rachel was kidnapped.

"Mims, the map," said Pops.

Mims spread a large map of the UK on the table.

"Rachel, a pin please."

"And blindfold her, please Astrid."

"Now, spin her around and guide her back to the map."

"Go Rachel! Stick the pin in!"

"Hmmm, Derbyshire," mused Pops looking at where the pin had landed. "I wonder if we'd be able to find jobs nearby, if we can get the girls into a good school and find us the perfect house?"

"There's only one way to find out," laughed Mims. "It's time to plan a Half Term break."

Unbeknownst to the girls, Pops and Mims did some research into the area in which the pin had landed. They found that the large city of Sheffield bordered onto Derbyshire's Peak District and actually had two universities for them to try to get jobs in. They discovered that a delightful little market town of Bakewell, famed for its' puddings, was within easy reach of Sheffield.

And so it was that during the Autumn Half Term holiday the Smith-Hyde family piled into the Range Rover and heading up north on the M1 motorway, took the exit that signposted 'Chesterfield.' Another 15 minutes took them into a car park beside a cattle market. Stretching their stiff legs, they headed over a bridge than led them over a little river teeming with ducks and moor hens and found themselves with a choice of direction. To the right a path alongside the river led to the town. To the left the path led to beautiful open parkland edged by a few pretty houses. They chose the left hand lane and as they strolled beside the river, they admired the little houses all with pretty names. The last one, named 'Palings', sat facing a cricket green and had the most wonderful sign at the front gate:

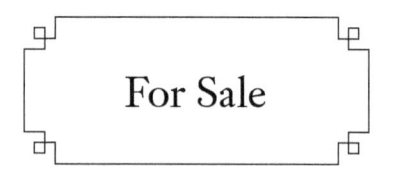

> For Sale

This was just the start of a busy few days in Derbyshire for the Smith-Hyde family. Pops and Mims both had successful interviews at the universities in Sheffield – just a few miles away. They met the Headmistress of a well respected school, right there in Bakewell who was happy to take the girls. Finally, they met with the Estate Agent

Rachel's Changes

and put in an offer on Palings. The choice of the pin in the map had been perfect.

As a tired family slowly started the drive back south to arrange selling Mulberry Cottage and planning their move, Pops reminded the family of a promise he had made to Rachel, "We will make a proper visit to the Tower of London before we leave the south of England".

"Mims commented, "And I'll need to buy new car."

"And we'll need to get a dog," laughed two happy girls.

As the car took them southwards the happy family took turns in choosing songs to sing. The miles melted away as they all looked forward to a peaceful new life, free from the threat of Ivan Barrowovski.

"I wonder where the house name of Palings comes from?" Rachel thought aloud.

"Ask Wanda the Wonder Girl!" giggled Astrid.

Lightning Source UK Ltd.
Milton Keynes UK
UKHW041843010419
340295UK00001B/18/P